THIS BOOK BELONGS TO:

Celebrate Kipper's 18th birthday
with other Kipper books:

Kipper
Kipper's Toybox
Kipper's Birthday
Kipper's Monster
Kipper and Roly
Kipper's Beach Ball

Storyboards:

Butterfly	Castle
Hisssss!	Miaow!
Honk!	Playtime!
Splosh!	Swing!

Visit www.hodderchildrens.co.uk/Kipper
for fun and games

Rocket

Mick Inkpen

Hodder Children's Books

A division of Hachette Children's Books

Tiger was sitting in the middle of the floor surrounded by odd shapes.

'It's my rocket!' he said proudly to Kipper. 'I've been waiting for it to come for weeks!'

The rocket was very complicated. At first, Tiger put all the bits together the wrong way round.

It took them all morning to get it right.

'Let's take it to the top of Big Hill!' said Kipper.

Everything was set.
Tiger was ready to
begin the countdown.

'Wait!' said Kipper.
'There's something missing.'
He ran to fetch Sock Thing,
and put it on the rocket.

'Every rocket
needs an
astronaut!'
he said.

'Ten, nine, eight, seven, six, five, four, three two, one!'

Nothing happened. Tiger had forgotten to pull out the aerial on the control box.

He tried again.

BOOM! The rocket
whizzed up into the sky!

'So what happens next?' said Kipper.

Tiger wasn't sure.

'Wait for it to come back, I suppose,' he said.

Kipper began to wonder whether he would ever see Sock Thing again.

They wandered off to the duck pond.

Pig and Arnold
were feeding the ducks.
'We've just fired a rocket
to the moon!' said Tiger.
'Really?' said Pig.
They were so busy telling
Pig about the rocket that
they didn't notice
Arnold pointing
up at the sky.

'Will your rocket
come back?' said Pig.
'I hope so,' said Tiger.
'I'm not sure really.'

Behind Pig, Sock Thing
floated gently down into
Arnold's hands.

Kipper was pleased to see Sock Thing again, and Tiger was pleased to have his rocket back.

Pig couldn't wait to see it go up again.

'Can I press the button?' he said, as they hurried off to Big Hill. 'Can I, Tiger? Can I?'